D1254330

Christmas Night
Fair and Bright

BY JULIE STIEGEMEYER

ILLUSTRATED BY MELISSA IWAI

CONCORDIA PUBLISHING HOUSE • SAINT LOUIS

Published 2007 by Concordia Publishing House
3558 S. Jefferson Avenue
St. Louis, MO 63118-3968
1-800-325-3040 • www.cph.org

Text © 2007 Julie Stiegemeyer

Illustrations © 2007 Concordia Publishing House

All rights reserved. No part of this publication may be reproduced,
stored in a retrieval system, or transmitted, in any form or by any
means, electronic, mechanical, photocopying, recording, or otherwise,
without the prior written permission of Concordia Publishing House.

Manufactured in China

1 2 3 4 5 6 7 8 9 10   16 15 14 13 12 11 10 09 08 07

For Marilyn Beyer and all of my English teachers

who taught me to love words.

J. S.

For the wonderful faculty and staff

at Grace Church School.

M. I.

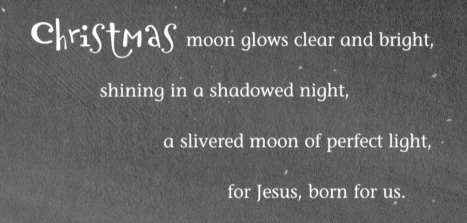

Christmas moon glows clear and bright,

shining in a shadowed night,

a slivered moon of perfect light,

for Jesus, born for us.

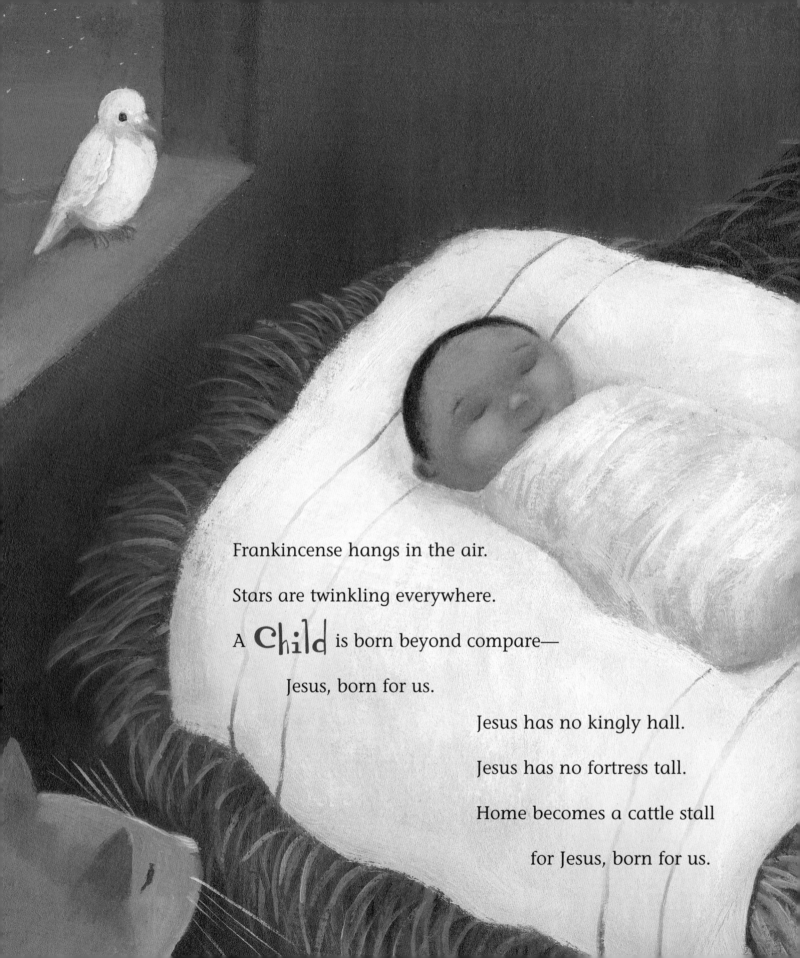

Frankincense hangs in the air.

Stars are twinkling everywhere.
A **Child** is born beyond compare—

Jesus, born for us.

Jesus has no kingly hall.

Jesus has no fortress tall.

Home becomes a cattle stall

for Jesus, born for us.

So sequined Stars shine as a crown,

night, a robe to wrap around;

God's own Son to earth came down.

He's Jesus, born for us.

Mary, mother, holds her Son:

promised Savior, holy One.

In Him God's rescue has begun.

He's Jesus, born for us.

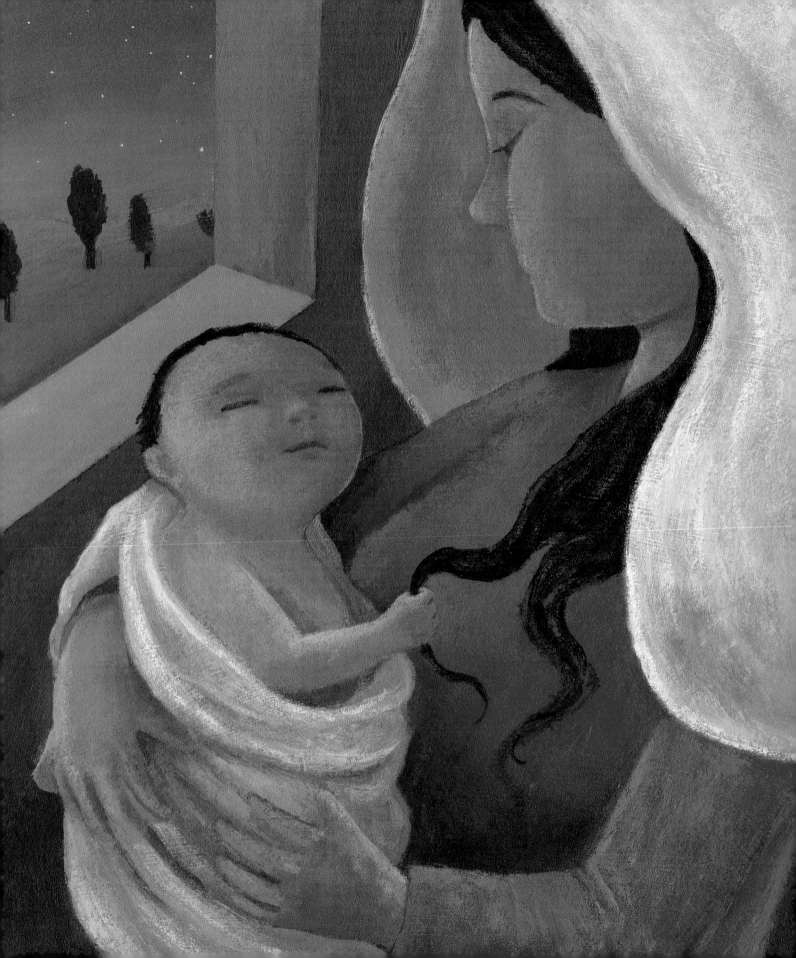

Hay-filled trough serves as a bed,

cradling His tiny head.

"Gloria!" the angels said

of Jesus, born for us.

Sent by angels to this place,

shepherds see a Child's face,

Child of mercy, Child of grace:

Jesus, born for us.

Angel's warning comes at **Night**

in Joseph's dreamy, sleepy sight,

"Flee from here before the light!"

Take Jesus, born for us.

Into Egypt off they go,

to a land they do not know.

Safely will the Child grow.

He's Jesus, born for us.

Through the **Shimmering** desert heat

on tired, dusty, dirty feet,

they plod on, no friends to greet,

with Jesus, born for us.

Days stretch on in desert sand

until the angel's firm command:

"Go back to Israel's holy land;

take Jesus, born for us."

Egypt moon glows fair and bright,

guides the way in shadowed night,

shines, a globe of perfect light,

for Jesus, born for us.

Born our Savior, born to cry,

born to suffer, born to die.

All our sin on Him will lie,

on Jesus, born for us.

At CHRISTMAS gathered in this place,
though we don't see our Savior's face,
we hear God's precious words of grace
of Jesus, born for us.

Christmas moon glows fair and bright,

shining now with Christmas light.

We celebrate His birth tonight:

Our Jesus, born for us.